llama llama loves to read

by **Anna Dewdney** and **Reed Duncan**
illustrated by **JT Morrow**

VIKING

Llama Llama learns at school.
Counting, writing, reading, rules.

Friends and school—
there's nothing better.
Llama learning all the letters!

Letters make a special set.
That set is called the **alphabet.**

Llama knows the first one, two, three.
He can say them—**A, B, C!**
And then there's **D.**
And next an **E.**
And on it goes to **X, Y, Z!**

No two letters are the same,
but every **letter** has a name:
It can be said. It can be heard.

Letters together make a **word.**

Llama Llama learning words.
Some he's seen and
some he's heard.
Some he has to memorize
with his brain and
with his eyes.

Llama Llama knows that one!
He can read it—this is **fun!**

Llama Llama writes his name.

And once again, just the same.
First **L**, then **l**, then **a-m-a.**

What do all these letters say . . . ?

Something to make
a present of.
L-o-v-e, that spells
LOVE!

Words make rhythm.
Words make rhyme.
Words make books for storytime.

Words tell truth.
Words tell new things.
Words make songs
that we can sing!

Words are the very best of presents.
Words together make a **sentence!**

Llama's hooves wave in the air.
Some words are hard—
it's just not fair!

No need to frown, no need to pout.
Just do your best and sound it out.

No need for crying,
moaning, bleating . . .

Llama Llama,
**HOORAY FOR
READING!**

Teacher holds the walking sign.
Now it's time to make a line.

How does Llama Llama know?
G and O spell **Go! Go! Go!**

Lots of sentences—take a look!—
strung together make a **book**.

Look inside: Oh, what glory!
All those words have made a **story!**

Llama reads so many things:
Fairy princess, pirate kings,

shiny knights and dragon fights,
under seas and up great heights.

Back to class, and off they go
filled with all the words they know.
Skipping, hopping, walk in line.
Llama Llama sees a sign.

And on that sign what does he see?
One **S**, one **T**, one **O**, one **P**.

Llama knows that word says **STOP.**
No more skipping! No more hops!

Llama reads the word out loud. Llama Llama feeling **PROUD!**

School is over. The day is done.
Llama had a lot of fun.

Words have magic power indeed.

Llama Llama loves to read.

VIKING
Penguin Young Readers
An imprint of Penguin Random House LLC
375 Hudson Street
New York, New York 10014

First published in the United States of America by Viking,
an imprint of Penguin Random House LLC, 2018

LIBRARY OF CONGRESS CATALOGING-IN-PUBLICATION DATA IS AVAILABLE
ISBN 9780670013975

Printed in China

1 3 5 7 9 10 8 6 4 2

Closely following the style of Anna Dewdney, the art for this book was created
with oil paint, colored pencil, and oil pastel on primed canvas.

To Azinda, my daughter, for all the bedtime
stories we read together. —J.T.M.

For librarians and all teachers of reading.
—A.D. & R.D.

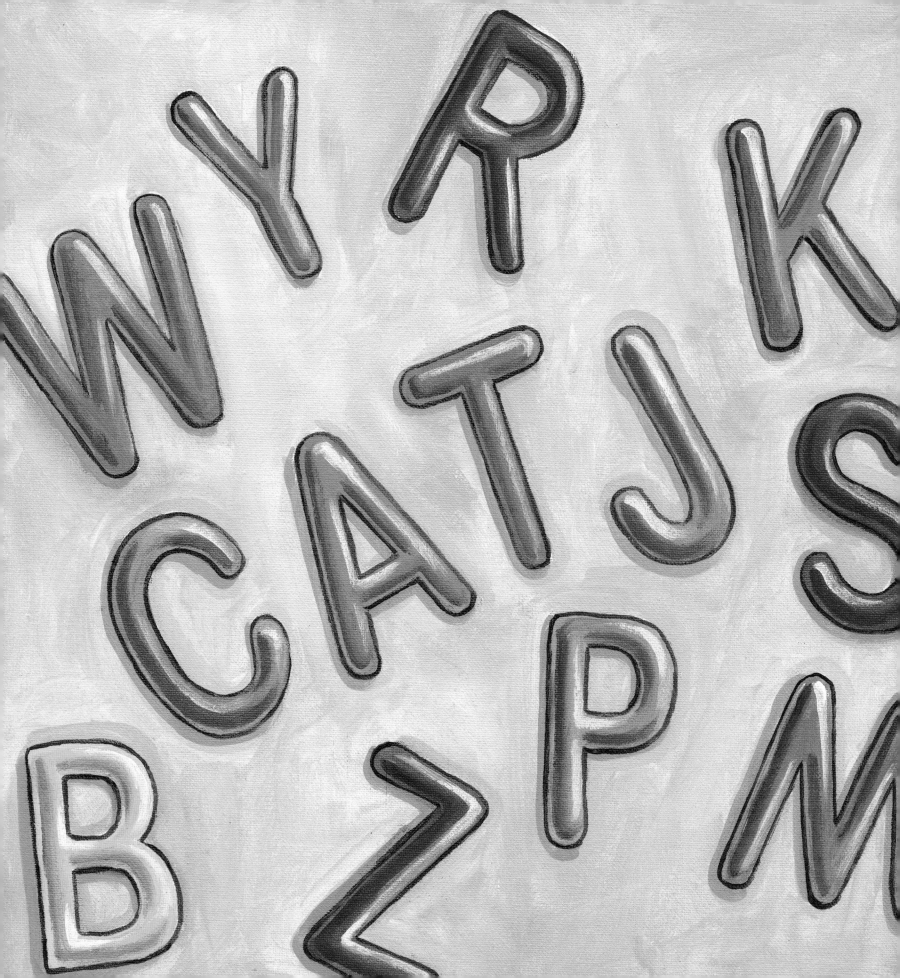